jellybeans

jellybeans

by Sylvia van Ommen

A Neal Porter Book
ROARING BROOK PRESS
Brookfield, Connecticut

Text copyright © 2002 by Sylvia van Ommen

English translation by Nancy Forest-Flier

A Neal Porter Book

Published by Roaring Brook Press,

Roaring Brook Press is a division of Holtzbrinck Publishing Holdings Limited Partnership,

2 Old New Milford Road, Brookfield, Connecticut 06804

First published in the Netherlands by Lemniscaat in 2002

Distributed in Canada by H. B. Fenn and Company Ltd.

Library of Congress Cataloging-in-Publication Data

Ommen, Sylvia Van.

[Drops. English]

Jellybeans / written and illustrated by Sylvia van Ommen.—1st ed.

P. cm.

"A Neal Porter Book."

Summary: Two friends, a rabbit and a cat, speculate about what heaven

will be like as they enjoy a visit to the park.

ISBN 1-59643-035-4

[1. Heaven—Fiction. 2. Rabbits—Fiction. 3. Cats—Fiction. 4. Friendship—Fiction.]   I. Title.

PZ7.O54855 Je 2004   [E]—dc22   2003018137

Roaring Brook Press books are available for special promotions and premiums.

For details contact: Director of Special Markets, Holtzbrinck Publishers.

First American edition 2004

2   4   6   8   10   9   7   5   3   1

Printed in the United States of America

Hi. Have you seen how nice it is outside? How about going to the park to eat jellybeans? Bye, Oscar.
P.S. You bring the jellybeans.

O.K. See you later. Bye, George.
P.S. You bring the drinks.

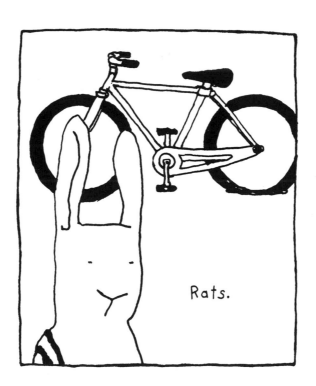

He speeds ahead, leaving his pursuers far behind. He's outsmarted them once again.

I'm almost there.   I had a flat tire.

What kind of jellybeans have you got?

A bag of mixed ones.

Hot chocolate.

Great.

I brought some sugar, too.

This one is as blue as the sky.

Do you think . . .

Up there . . .

Do you think there's a heaven up there?

A place you go when you're dead?

I don't know. I think so.

Will we go there, too—
both of us?

I'm going if you're going, that's for sure.

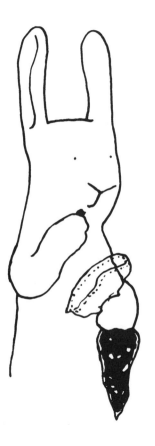

We might bump into
each other there.

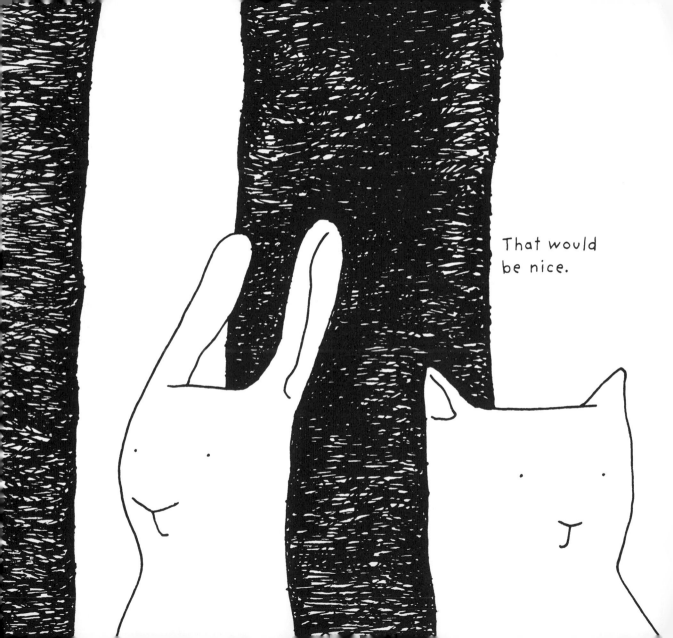

That would
be nice.

But what if it's really big and you never bump into anybody?

We can agree to meet at the entrance . . .

Or at one of those
special meeting places.

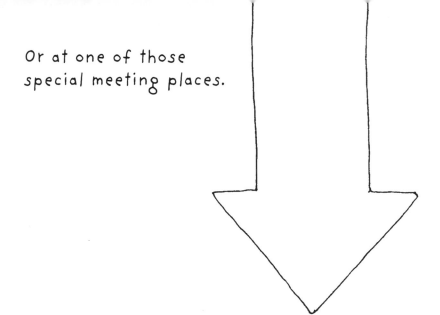

Wow, that was fast!   Hey!

But maybe we won't know each other when we get there.

What do you mean?

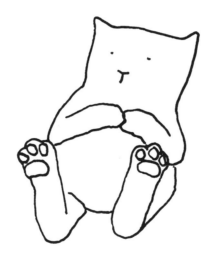

Well, because maybe when we're dead we will have forgotten everything we ever did.

Then there's no sense meeting at the entrance.

But if we bump into each other
and we don't recognize each other . . .

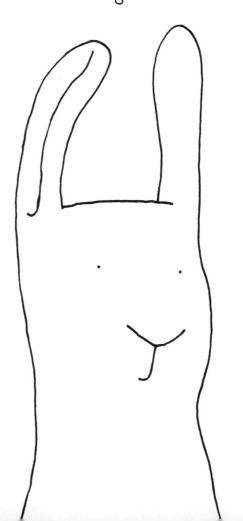

Then we can just become friends all over again.

Eat jellybeans together, stuff like that . . .

Great.